JUNGLE DOCTOR'S FABLES

①

JUNGLE DOCTOR'S FABLES

Paul White
CF4·K

10 9 8 7 6 5 4 3 2 1

Jungle Doctor's Fables ISBN 978-1-84550-608-7

© Copyright 1955 Paul White

First published 1955. Reprinted eight times.

Paperback edition 1972. Revised 1984,

Reprinted 1986, 1988, 1990, 1995

Published in 2010 by

Christian Focus Publications, Geanies House, Fearn, Tain,

Ross-shire, IV20 1TW, Scotland, U.K.

Paul White Productions,

4/1-5 Busaco Road, Marsfield, NSW 2122, Australia

Cover design: Daniel van Straaten

Cover illustration: Andy Robb

Interior illustrations: Graham Wade

Printed and bound by Bell and Bain, Glasgow

Mixed Sources

Product group from well-managed
forests and other controlled sources
www.fsc.org Cert no. TT-COC-002769
© 1996 Forest Stewardship Council

FSC

Scripture quotations are either the author's own paraphrase
or are taken from The New Testament in Modern English,
copyright © 1958, 1959, 1960
J.B. Phillips and 1947, 1952, 1955, 1957
The Macmillian Company, New York.
Used by permission. All rights reserved.

CONTENTS

INTRODUCTION

Paul White learned a great deal from his African friends at the jungle hospital. They befriended him and helped him in his efforts to learn their language, Chigogo.

One of their most important gifts was to teach him how to use animal stories. These stories, or fables, helped to explain abstract thoughts and theological terms.

When the Whites were on their way home from Africa in 1941, they were delayed in Colombo because of German submarine activity. Paul was invited to speak at a girls' boarding school. All the children of non-Christian faiths were sent outside but, hearing laughter from inside, crowded round the windows to see what they were missing. This was the first of many occasions when audiences were gripped by the fable stories.

The first of six fable books appeared in 1955. A menagerie of African animals is used to teach the gospel and how to live the Christian life. In these books you will meet Toto, the mischievous monkey, Boohoo, the hippo who, like the author, suffered from allergies, Twiga, the giraffe and wise teacher, and many others.

They will endear themselves to you as they have to thousands round the globe.

1
MONKEY, MIRROR AND RED PAINT

The camp fire burned brightly under the hospital buyu tree. A large mirror reflected its glow on many eager faces.

Daudi, Jungle Doctor's assistant, pointed to it. 'My story is about mirrors – this sort and the special one that shows what you're like inside.'

Once upon a jungle morning Toto, the small monkey, found a paint tin. He grabbed it and scampered off chuckling with glee. He liked the smell of it. He liked the squelchy noise it made. He liked the red streaks on the side of it. Contentedly he sat down under an umbrella tree making happy noises as he wondered what was inside.

Twiga, the giraffe, watched him battling with the lid. He turned to Hippo. 'Here's trouble.'

'*Um – yes*,' nodded Boohoo. 'Be careful, little monkey. There can be things in tins like that. If I were you ...'

'You're not,' laughed Toto, 'and you never will be.' He shouted with joy as he wrenched off the lid. He sniffed. 'Smells like nuts.'

Giraffe knew the worst had happened when he saw Toto's head disappear into the paint pot as far as his ears would let it. Slowly a paint-covered monkey face re-appeared. Toto knew something strange had happened, but no matter how he rolled his eyes he couldn't see what it was.

'Your tongue tells you it's not good to eat,' said Twiga, 'but your eyes haven't the chance to tell you how odd your face is.'

Toto sniffed. 'My face is all right.'

'Look at it and you'll see what I mean,' smiled Twiga.

A drop of red paint dripped from Monkey's nose. He looked startled. 'How can I look at my own face?'

Twiga bent down his long neck. 'Go to the place near the *buyu* tree. Inside you'll find a shining sort of window called *mirror*. Look into it and you'll look back at yourself and see what's wrong.'

Toto blinked, nodded and scuttled off. No-one was about. There was the *buyu* tree. There was the door. And there was the shining thing. He tip-toed in and was about to peer into it when someone shouted at him and started to throw stones.

Toto bolted through the thornbush, over great rocks and between the trunks of big trees. At last he stopped, panting, under a large and spiky cactus. He glanced into the mirror and caught a glimpse of a monkey with an absurdly red face. He took no notice. He'd never look like that!

Holding the mirror against his chest Toto scampered up the *buyu* tree. Simba, the lion, came striding up the path. He seldom even noticed monkeys but today he stopped and stared at Toto and the mirror. Lion tossed his mane and growled, 'Look into it and use it.'

Toto was proud that Simba had noticed him. He swung from a limb in the sunlight and his monkey fancy was tickled by a sparkling patch of light as he wiggled the mirror to and fro. 'Look into it?' he gurgled. 'Not on your monkey life. I'm going to have fun with this.'

Boohoo, the hippo, eased himself out of his favourite water-lily pond and strolled under the *buyu* tree dripping mud at every step. He stopped, looked up at Toto and said, '*Um*, little monkey, your face is red. That thing you're holding could help you to – *um* – see what a mess it really is.' Toto shone the patch of light into Hippo's eyes.

'You don't need anything to help you see what a mess you are.'

'Stop doing that,' spluttered Hippo, blinking his eyes and wrinkling his nose. '*Er*, look out, I'm – *um* – going to ...' A huge hippo sneeze boomed and echoed through the jungle.

Monkey was delighted. He chuckled and danced up and down. He dazzled Suku, the parrot, who flew round and round him. 'Look into it, Toto. Mirrors aren't to play with. Look into it. Your face,' screeched Suku, 'it's dirty, dirty, dirty. If I had a face like yours I wouldn't want to look at it either.'

Twiga came close behind him. 'Toto, you ball of mischief. Have you forgotten what's happened to you? As Suku says, mirrors are made to look into, not to play with. They're to show you yourself as you really are and what to do about it.'

Small monkey made a rude face at Twiga and scuttled off to sit on an ant hill. In the tall grass below, Hyena winked at him and whispered, 'Monkey, take no notice of old long neck, you're a big monkey now. Do your own thing. You show 'em. If it feels good, do it. That's what I say. But don't look into that mirror thing whatever you do.'

Toto blinked and bit his nails.

'I'll tell you what,' coaxed Hyena. 'Wrap it up in a banana leaf and put it where it won't get in your way. Don't worry about what's on your face. It will wear off in time.' Monkey heard muffled laughter as Hyena crept back to his lair in the swamp.

At that moment a banana skin fell – *flop* – beside him. He looked up and saw his uncle Nyani sitting on his favourite limb happily eating. Toto moved the mirror. Blinding light struck monkey uncle's eyes. He shaded them with his paw to find out what was happening. In the glare he saw Toto and heard him giggle.

Slowly and deliberately Nyani peeled an overripe banana. His hairy arm shot out – WHAM! Toto staggered, tripped and fell, his face covered with bad banana as well as the red paint. Making grumpy noises Uncle Nyani climbed down the *buyu* tree. Hyena laughed and laughed as he heard the sounds of monkey misery mixed with the thump of a hard paw on the softer end of unhappy Toto.

Giraffe walked quietly to the place where Toto stood letting the cool breeze blow on his less comfortable parts. 'Small monkey,' he said, 'what is the good of a mirror unless you use it and use it properly? I'll tell you again. It's not a toy. It will show you yourself as you really are.'

Toto slowly raised the mirror and looked into it. He frowned and a face, spattered with banana and smeared with paint, frowned back at him. He gasped and scurried down to the water.

14

Some time later, one corner of the water-lily pond had streaks of yellow and red in its shallow parts and a rather wet Toto hurried back to Giraffe. He picked up the mirror again and looked carefully into it.

'Well done,' said Twiga. 'The mirror told you the truth and you did the wise thing.'

Boohoo nodded his great head. '*Um* – useful things, mirrors.'

Daudi smiled. 'Here in my pocket is an even more useful mirror. With ordinary ones you can see your outside, but with this one you can find out what's going on inside you: deep inside your head and in your heart.'

'And,' chuckled Mboga, Daudi's right-hand man, 'we all know that it is God's book.'

'Truly,' said Daudi, 'and when you look into it you will see how your sin can be forgiven. After that your happiness and usefulness as a Christian depends on how thoroughly you use the great mirror, and how carefully you do what it shows you.'

He flicked over the pages of his Bible. 'Listen to James chapter 1, verse 25: "The person who looks into the perfect mirror of God's law and makes a habit of doing so is not the one who sees and forgets. That person does what God's word tells him to do and wins true happiness".'

* * *

What's Inside the Fable?

Special Message: The Bible is God's mirror. Use it, obey it and change your life.

'How can a young person keep his life clean? By living according to your word' *Psalm 119 verse 9.*

You will find over 100 things in *Psalm 119* that God's Word can do for you.

2
THE GREAT WALL

Drums beat in the African night. At the jungle hospital the camp fire was crackling cheerfully, lighting up the faces of the people who sat under the buyu tree.

Mgogo, a sturdy boy, brought a three-legged stool and put it in the light of the fire. 'Bwana Daudi, you pray and say you talk to God but when I try it's like talking to ...' – he looked across towards a place where a new ward was being built – '... it's like talking to a great stone wall.'

'Talking of walls,' said Daudi, 'who is building that one?'

'I am,' replied Mabwe, the stone mason. 'I put in every stone and every bit of mortar and it's solid.'

'Right,' nodded Daudi. 'Walls are the trouble. We need to know what to do about them. Now listen to my story.'

Once upon a jungle day the animals had no joy to find that they were cut off from the best parts of the jungle by a huge wall. It blocked their way to the greenest grass, the shadiest trees and the clear springs of water.

'Twiga Giraffe,' rumbled Rhino, 'you're the tallest. What do you see?'

From round him sounded angry growling and grumbling noises. Loudest was the sad voice of Boohoo, the hippo.

'*Um ... er*, that thing stops me from seeing the great river and the lovely cool pools and the delicious mud to lie in. It – *um ...*'

Giraffe stood on the tips of his hooves. 'It's the biggest wall I've ever seen. It's high and it's thick and it seems to go on and on.'

'We're in trouble,' groaned Stripey, the zebra. 'This side is dry and dusty – it's desert.'

'It's disaster,' roared Rhino. His little eyes were red. He stamped his great feet. 'So we're blocked off from the best places, eh? Blocked off! And all you can do is talk. *Do something*. DO SOMETHING.'

'*Um*, yes,' nodded Hippo. '*Er*, like what?'

'Like this!' thundered Rhino. 'I'll crash through it. Get out of my way.'

The horn on his nose pointed like a spear. He tossed his head.

'Great wall, *heh*? Watch me go through it!'

Rhino charged. The faster he ran, the more the ground shook. Two tons of raging rhino hurtled towards the wall – closer – closer – *Wham* – BANG – THUMP. The trees trembled. Dust rose in clouds. He staggered back and collapsed, dazed and dizzy. His front feet clutched his buckled horn. Each of his beady eyes peered in a different direction. On his forehead a bruise became bigger and bigger while his mind spun like a whirlwind. But the great wall stood exactly as it was before.

'That wall has huge strength,' muttered Giraffe.

'*Mmm*,' remarked Hippo. 'Yes. It seems to be – *um* – rather thick.'

Groaning noises came from Rhino's swollen lips. 'There's no way through that wall.'

The animals looked at one another and echoed, 'There's no way through that wall.'

Boohoo nodded. 'No way through.'

The lips of Mbisi, the hyena, curled and he half-sniggered, half-snarled. 'For those with big feet and small brains there is a problem.' He sneered at Rhino and Hippo. 'Wisdom, not weight, is what you want. No, watch cunning hyena find a way *round* it.'

Giraffe peered at the great wall that stretched far into the heat haze. 'We will watch you with interest.'

Hyena slunk off. They could hear his ugly sniggering till he was out of sight.

Hours and hours later, when the shadows were growing long, Twiga called, 'Here he comes.' They watched Mbisi return, limping and weary-footed. He flopped down and whimpered. 'It's useless. It goes on and on and on. There's no way around it.'

'*Um* – yes,' remarked Boohoo, raising one eyebrow. 'No way round it, *eh*?' He blinked. 'That means – *um* – no way *through*, no way *round*.'

Softly Snake slid off his warm rock. 'Legs,' he hissed scornfully, his head swaying. 'Legs won't get you to the other side. You animals of strength and so-called wisdom have all failed. But I, Nzoka, the snake, with my splendid supple spine – I can find a way *under* the wall.'

20

He coiled and uncoiled his long shiny body and disappeared down a hole near the bottom of the wall. The animals waited and watched.

After a while Toto, the monkey, scuttled across to the warm flat stone. 'He's under there, squirming this way and that.' He did a monkey pantomime of Snake travelling underground.

'He's sliding here and sliding there – creeping up and creeping down, turning this way and twisting that. He's slithering ...'

'Er, look out, Monkey,' bellowed Hippo.

There was a small puff of dust near the wall. Snake's head shot out of a hole. He was facing the wall. His tongue flicked in and out with triumph. 'I've done it! I'm on the other side.'

Toto's giggle interrupted him. 'Gently, now, Supple Spine. You're still here with us.'

Nzoka's head nodded in anger. Poison dripped from his fangs. 'There is no way *under* the wall or I, Snake, would have found it.'

Boohoo smiled. '*Er*, quite so. I'm rather glad there is no – *um* – way under that wall. It would be rather a tight fit for hippos, I – *er* – think.' He raised both his eyebrows. 'And that means no way *through* the wall, no way *round* the wall, no way *under* the wall.'

It was at that moment that Toto had his great idea. 'Why didn't you tell me. I, Monkey, can climb anything, *anything*. I'll climb *over* that wall. Twiga, stand close and give me a helping neck and I'll be over in a jiffy.'

Monkey took some deep breaths, did some exercises and shouted, 'Watch, everybody. Here we go!'

He grabbed Twiga's tail, swung on to his back, swarmed up his long neck, scrambled on to his head and leapt up – front paws clutching the wall, back paws clutching the wall and tail helping wherever it could.

'*Er*, do you think he'll do it?' gulped Hippo.

But the higher the wall went the smoother it became. Monkey slowed, clutching with his front paws, groping with his back paws, his tail swinging uselessly. For a split second he was still and then – down, down, down he somersaulted to land THUMP! at Twiga's feet.

Winded and shocked, Monkey lay there. Giraffe did artificial respiration with the tip of his long nose. Slowly Toto's eyes opened. He propped himself against Boohoo's leg. He blinked, held his aching head and gasped out, 'No way *over* that wall. No way over ...'

'*Um,*' said Boohoo looking down at him. 'Then there's no way at all, little monkey. No way **through**, or **round**, or **under**, or **over** that great wall. None at all.'

All the animals stood sadly under the leafless *buyu* tree and, with understanding them, they looked at the big letters on the wall.

A chorus of glum voices came:

'No way **through** –

No way **round** –

No way **under** –

or **over** that great wall.'

Daudi stopped and looked at the faces of those who listened.

'The good news is that for you and me there is a way.'

Mgogo jumped to his feet and demanded, 'Why did God build that great wall to block us off from him?'

Mabwe, the stone mason, put his hand on his shoulder. 'We each build our own wall. Every stone of it, every bucket full of mortar – we build it with our own sin. We have shut ourselves off from God.'

'Truly,' said Daudi. 'Our pride, our selfishness, our lies and cheating, our spite and dirty-mindedness – this is sin and sin walls us off from God. Everyone everywhere has great wall trouble.

'Some try to quarry through that sin barrier. Some go on and on all their lives hoping they'll find a way round it. Some try to tunnel under the sin barrier and still others think up clever ways of climbing over the sin barrier. But none of them works.

'Jesus himself said, "No one comes to the father but by me." and he made a way. With his cross he broke through the great wall.

'You and I would be in a hopeless position if he hadn't done that. And he says, "Come to me. I am come that you may have and enjoy life to the full."

'If you find yourself on the wrong side of the wall and you want to get through to God, Jesus has the answer. He said, "I am the way."'

* * *

What's Inside the Fable?

Special Message: Jesus is the only way to the Father.

Read *John chapter 14 verses 1 to 7.*

Read the adventure of John, Peter and a crippled man in *Acts chapter 3 verse 1* through *to Acts chapter 4 verse 12.*

3

WHY GOD SENT JESUS

Young Mdimi, the herd boy, shuddered. 'It was a lion that attacked me. Yoh! His claws and his teeth ...' He pulled the sheet over his head.

It was in the children's ward of the Jungle Doctor hospital. From the next bed Goha smiled. 'But the Bwana says the bite I received was much more dangerous.'

'Yoh,' sniffed Mdimi. 'It was only a mosquito that bit you.'

'Eheh, but the Bwana says mosquitoes kill millions of people every year – and lions only hundreds.'

The door opened and in came Daudi, his arms full of home-made Christmas decorations. The boys watched him loop coloured paper round the walls and hang up sparkling silver balls that made the windows come alive and twinkle.

Daudi asked, 'How is your shoulder and arm, Mdimi?'

'Stiff, Bwana, but not sore unless I move it. But yoh!' His eyes opened wide as Mboga staggered in with the limb of a pepper tree in a kerosene tin. He looked round the small ward. 'Why do all this?'

'We're preparing for the birthday of the Lord Jesus Christ. God sent him to earth nearly two thousand years ago. Christmas is a time of rejoicing.'

Mdimi nodded. 'I have heard; and there is a feast, much rice and goat stew.' He propped himself up on one elbow and said, 'Bwana Daudi, why did God send Jesus?'

Daudi smiled down at the two eager boys. 'Listen, both of you, and then you'll understand.'

Behold, everyone in this part of the country knows my dog, Chibwa, a small animal with a cheerful face and a lively tail. In the days of the first rains Chibwa and I went to my garden to plant peanuts. He had great joy. He frisked about, chased lizards, barked at birds, and his nose found many interesting smells.

On the path were lion's footprints. Chibwa sniffed cautiously and then wagged his tail as if to say, 'All is well. None of the fierce ones of the jungle have passed this way for many days.'

We came to my garden and I sang a work song as I laboured with my hoe. Chibwa also dug with his back legs. There was that lovely smell of moist earth. I shaped the soil into ridges.

Little dog sat there watching. I smiled at him. 'Chibwa, soon I'm going to plant peanuts. As the rains fall these will grow and in the time of harvest we will fill bags and bags with them. Then, in the days of great heat and no rain when nothing grows, we will have food to strengthen us and keep life going within our skins.'

Chibwa put his head on one side, wagged his tail, and I thought. Is he not an animal of wisdom? Inside his head the whole matter is clear. I planted two rows, covering each peanut with brown earth but out of the corner of my eye I saw Chibwa digging up the nuts, chewing them and pushing the empty shells out of his mouth with his busy red tongue.

I went over to him and said, 'Small dog.' He looked up at me and both his eyes and tail talked joy. In a friendly voice I said. 'Let me tell you again. If you dig up the seed there'll be no harvest. I will starve and because of that so will you. There is no profit, small dog, in digging up what I plant, so please don't do it.'

He wagged his tail and I thought, I have spoken with kindness and have explained things with gentleness. Now, behold, all will be well. Surely this is the way to make things clear to dogs.

Next day we went happily to the garden. Bees buzzed round the big white flowers of the *buyu* tree and Chibwa yapped cheerfully. And again I dug and planted. For a time Chibwa watched me then he trotted over to the place where I had started and with busy feet dug up peanut after peanut.

I threw down my hoe. 'Chibwa, come here! *Come here!*' I slapped him firmly. In surprise he yelled. His tail went sorrowfully between his legs. There was no joy in his eyes.

'Dog,' I said, and there was moderate fierceness in my tone. 'Dig up those peanuts and there will be no harvest and that could mean the end of both of us.'

Then I stroked his ears. 'Please, my Chibwa, please understand.'

As I went on digging I thought, 'That small amount of firmness will make the difference.'

The third day we set out again. The sun shone, the birds sang and I with them. In my bag was a bone, a large juicy bone. The words of my song were: 'It is a good thing to reward those who understand and obey.' Chibwa pranced around and I said, 'It's a thing of satisfaction that every word I speak is clear to you, tail-wagger. And to show you that it pays to obey, here ...'

I held out the bone and smiled at him. '*This* will help you to remember that bones are food for dogs – not miserable little peanuts that have much shell and only little food in them. Leave the seed, small dog, leave it where it will grow, and then there'll be food for us later on and more bones for *you*.'

His eyes smiled at me and his tail wagged with strength and I murmured to the bag of peanuts, 'The way of kindness works. At last I have brought light to his mind.'

On the final day of planting I was full of hope. Chibwa barked and raced through the bush. Then my heart sank. We had arrived at my garden and my little dog hurried to where I had planted the day before *and started to dig up the peanuts.*

My mind was in a whirl. How shall I make Chibwa understand? I sighed an unhappy sigh. For Chibwa is my small dog and my heart is warm towards him. I went and sat down under the *buyu* tree and thought many thoughts:

I've explained the whole problem to him and been very patient.

I've been severe.

I've given gifts. In every way I've tried to make him understand and it *doesn't* work. What can I do now?

Then I saw it all. There IS a way – only one way. I must become a dog and talk to him in dog language, then I will explain it to him and thus he will understand.

Mdimi and Goha looked at each other with lifted eyebrows and Daudi smiled. 'Listen carefully and you both will understand also. God felt about me as I feel about my small dog. God loves everybody. For thousands of years people have been told about God. Many take no notice. In the days long ago, God sent wise ones who explained about himself with song and

with story and with words easily understood. But many, many people closed their ears.

'At last he said, "I will send my son." And this is what he did that first Christmas day. God became a man. He came to earth as a baby – to live and grow and laugh and suffer, just like we do. It's hard to understand God. He's everywhere. He's all-powerful. We can see what he does but we cannot see him.

'But it's different with Jesus. We can understand him because we know what a man looks like and feels like. The Bible explains it this way: "Jesus is the image of the invisible God."

'And He did more than show us God and feel what all of us feel. He took our place on the cross. We all deserve to be punished, but Jesus took our punishment.

'So when I try to think of God and my mind staggers, then I think of Jesus. I read the Bible and see how he taught and healed and how he died so that we could be forgiven; and to make it clear to us how deadly sin is.

'But he didn't just die and that was the end of it. He came back to life to prove he is God, to rescue us and to give us new life. These days God has spoken to us by his son.

'That's why God sent Jesus.'

Next morning Daudi greeted Jungle Doctor with a smile.

'Bwana, good news of happenings in the boys' ward. Mdimi's people have come to greet him. They *rejoice that he is recovering. They're all standing round his bed and what do you think he is doing?'*

'Tell me, Daudi.'

'Yoh! He has understood our words and he's telling them why God sent Jesus.'

* * *

What's Inside the Fable?

Special Message: Jesus came to show what God is like.

Jesus means: God saves.
This tells us *who he is* – God
and *what he does* – saves.

Read *Hebrews chapter 1 verses 1 to 3 and Colossians chapter 1 verses 15 to 20.*

4
MONKEY IN THE MUD

'No camp fire tonight,' laughed Mboga. 'After that thunderstorm there's nothing but mud.'

Daudi smiled as he lit two hurricane lanterns. 'These will do instead. We'll sit on the roots of the buyu tree and I'll tell a story about ...'

Mboga grinned, 'Mud?'

'Mud it is.'

'MUD,' muttered Boohoo, the hippo, '*um*, I'm very fond of mud. Restful and – *eh* – soothing it is.' He yawned and settled back comfortably among the water-lilies.

'Don't you ever get stuck in the mud?' asked Koko, the monkey, Nyani's sinewy nephew who often bragged about his strength and stamina.

'*Um* – no.' Little waves spread over the pond as Hippo shook his great head. 'That is, since Aunt Soso disappeared. She ...'

'What happened?' demanded the little monkey.

'*Um* – big she was, a rather large hippo and a bit – *um* – short-sighted. She wandered into that swamp called *Matope* – bad mud, slimy, squelchy – *um* – down-sucking mud. Be careful. It's ...'

But Koko sniffed and shrugged his shoulders. He had found a coconut. He threw it to Nyani and they scampered off, throwing it and catching it with skill. They scampered over the gardens where last year's corn stalks rotted. Tossing the big nut over small thorn trees and spiky cactus they came to the slope where *buyu* trees grew on the hillside that led down to the swamp. Here Nyani bumped into a wasps' nest.

'*Yow!*' he yelled as they stung him. He threw down the nut which rolled and bounced and bounded downhill to land *Plop!* In the middle of the place of slimy, sticky, down-sucking mud. The monkeys stood on the bank watching the coconut floating way out from the bank.

'I'll get it back,' shouted Koko.

'No, stop.' Nyani grabbed at him. 'It's too dangerous. It's Boohoo's big, bad, swamp. Don't ...'

But Koko pulled away from him. 'I'm strong. I'm nimble. Leave it to me. I know what I'm doing.' He raced downhill and jumped far out, landing *plomp* beside the nut.

He scooped it up. 'There you are. I did it. I'm no blundering old hippo. The coconut's safe and so is Koko.' He laughed and thumped his chest and turned to run back to the bank. But the swamp gripped his left foot.

Monkey wisdom told him, 'Push hard with the other foot.' He did. But before you could say coconut, both his feet had sunk to the ankles in the sticky, squelchy, down-sucking mud.

Daudi paused. 'Was it easy to get into the swamp?'

A score of heads nodded.

'Could he get out by himself?'

A score of shoulders shrugged.

'Monkey was in bad trouble,' went on Daudi, 'but he didn't realise it.'

Koko shouted, 'I'll be out in a tick.' He struggled with all his might but the mud rose further and further up his monkey shins.

Slowly into his monkey mind crept the horrible thought, 'It's got me!' he threw away the coconut and yelled, 'Uncle Nyani, help!' The monkey on the bank ran up and down scratching his head.

Koko was really scared. The more he struggled the more he sank. The more he sank the more he struggled and the mud crept up to his knees.

Then Nyani had his bright monkey idea. 'Koko,' he shouted. 'For one so young you have strong whiskers. Grasp yourself by those whiskers and *lift yourself out*. LIFT YOURSELF OUT!'

Koko chattered with joy. Surely now he was saved. He grabbed himself by the whiskers and lifted with all his strength. For a moment it seemed to work, but he was only taking the kinks out of his backbone. The mud climbed slowly. In despair Koko grasped his whiskers and pulled again.

Nyani ran up and down the bank screaming, 'Lift yourself out! Lift yourself out! Go on!' But the mud climbed and climbed, hair by hair, towards Koko's hips.

Daudi asked in a hushed voice. 'Was it easy to get into the swamp?'

'Eheh.'

'Could he get out by himself?'

'Ng'o.' They shook their heads.

'Is there any profit in being in a swamp and being sucked down?'

'Ng'ooo.' Their heads shook vigorously.

'And if he stays there long enough?'

A muttered chorus answered, 'Koh! A thing of sadness.'

Daudi sighed. 'It was a thing of no joy.'

Koko struggled with all his monkey might but it didn't help. He was going down and down and the mud was oozing up and up. Nyani dashed up and down, crying his useless monkey cry of, 'Lift yourself out.'

The mud pressed on his ribs. It climbed to the hollow under his neck. It reached the straining muscles of his arms. He panted as it covered his shoulders and gasped when it pressed on his throat.

There was a breathless hush. Daudi leaned forward. There was a long pause then he said, 'It happens to people too. Like Koko, I was in that swamp. What is its name?

'It's easy to get into.

'You can't get out of it by yourself.

'It makes you miserable all the time you're in it and in the end, it kills.'

The answer came from Mgulu, whose leg was in plaster. 'The name of the swamp must be sin, Bwana Daudi. But how can anyone escape?'

'Right. The great problem is how to get out. I tried to lift myself out by my whiskers for I thought that what I did could save me. But the more I struggled the more I sank. And then I saw someone on the bank. I did not see his face but I saw his hand stretched out to me and in that hand was a scar. He said, "Put your hand into mine and I will lift you out. I am the way."'

Mgulu's whisper came clearly, 'It was Jesus.'

Daudi nodded. 'But I thought, shall I do it? Can't I struggle on by myself and fight my way out? And then I felt the pull of the mud and I knew that those trapped in the swamp of sin died there. I understood that there was no way but Jesus so I gladly put my hand into his and strongly he pulled me out.'

One by one people moved away into the warm night. Mgulu lingered. He shivered. 'I hate to think of what happened to monkey ...'

Daudi put his hand on the boy's shoulder. 'True, but for you and me, think of who Jesus is, what Jesus did and what Jesus promises.'

* * *

What's Inside the Fable?

Special Message: You can't buy, earn or talk your way out of sin. You need to be rescued.

From fear to faith. *Ephesians chapter 2 verses 1 to 9* and *Colossians chapter 1 verses 13 and 14.*

5

THE MONKEYS WHO DIDN'T BELIEVE IN CROCODILES

'Let's make it a small camp fire tonight,' said Daudi. 'I don't want much light because this is a rather spooky story.

'But first, which would you rather be bitten by: a lion, a leopard, a snake, a hippo, or a crocodile?'

Mboga laughed. 'I'd rather not be bitten at all.'

Daudi chuckled. 'Good answer. Far better than the wisdom of the twin monkeys, Tip and Top.'

Uncle Nyani was furious. 'You monkey twins are a disgrace to our family tree!' He grabbed each of them by the scruff of the neck and banged their heads together. 'I've a good mind to drag you down to the river and throw you to the crocodile.'

The little monkeys struggled free, made faces at their uncle and said rudely, 'We don't believe in crocodiles. There're no such things as crocodiles.'

Nyani shook his fist at them. 'Crocodiles are fierce. They have beady eyes like python, mouths bigger than hippo, teeth sharper than leopard and tails as strong as elephant's trunk. And they live down by the river and more than anything else they love to eat little monkeys.'

The twins giggled. 'It's a yarn. They're not. It's all rot.' And then as they trotted off in the direction of the river they sang together:

He's only trying to scare us.
He's only trying to scare us.
He's only trying to scare us.
But we won't fall for that.

They hadn't gone far before they met Twiga, the giraffe. 'Twiga,' said Tip, 'from up there you see more than anybody else in the jungle. We have a question. Do you know a creature that loves to eat small monkeys, that walks on land and swims in water? He has little beady eyes with a mouth bigger than hippo's, teeth sharper than leopard's and a tail as strong as elephant's trunk.'

Twiga nodded his long neck. 'Why yes, that's Crocodile. Keep away from him. Do you remember that muscular monkey, Tuffy? He met a crocodile and ...'

The twins jeered in chorus, '*Hah*, became a crocodile's dinner, *eh*? Rot, bosh and rubbish. You're as bad as our uncle Nyani.' And away they trotted singing:

We don't believe in crocodiles,
There're no such things as crocodiles.

As they scampered on downhill they met Boohoo, the hippo.

'Boohoo,' said Top. 'You're a very wise animal. You know about rivers, lakes and pools of water. Do you know a sort of dragon with a mouth as big as yours, teeth sharper than leopard's, little beady eyes and a tail stronger than elephant's trunk?'

'*Um* – yes! Good description too. That's Crocodile, nasty beast – *um* – and dangerous, 'specially for monkeys. Eats 'em, you know.'

'Pish and tush!' sniffed Tip.

'Twaddle!' agreed Top. And they wandered on, singing their 'don't believe in' song.

They skipped round a big rock and there was Mbisi, the hyena, who had heard the 'no such thing as crocodiles' part.

'Quite right, too,' he scoffed. 'Don't you believe those yarns. You're smart monkeys. *Heh, heh, heh.*'

Tip felt uneasy prickles under his skin but he liked to be called smart so he said, 'Do you know about a great creature with beady eyes who …?'

'*Heh, heh, heh,*' Hyena laughed scornfully. 'Did it have teeth sharper than leopard, did they tell you that too?'

Tip nodded eagerly. 'Yes, and ...'

Hyena sniffed. 'Did they tell you about its huge mouth?'

'Yes, and they said ...'

'It had eyes like snake and a special joy in eating young monkeys, *eh?*'

'Yes, yes. How did you know, Hyena?'

Mbisi laughed creepily. 'Don't you believe them, monkeys. You're big enough now to go where you like and do what you like when you like. Show how smart you are. Tonight is full moon. Go down to the river and have a big laugh hunting for dragons in the moonlight. And take a look at the reflections in the water and see how good-looking you are, *heh, heh, heh.*'

Within sight of the water they stopped and looked anxiously about, but they felt better when they could see themselves mirrored in the calm water at the river's edge. They smiled and made faces, put out their tongues, wiggled their ears, and had all sorts of fun.

Top giggled. '*Crocodiles.* We were right. There aren't any crocodiles. It was all a yarn.'

'All twaddle and tush,' said Tip.

'All bosh and rubbish,' agreed Top.

Then the sun set and the water seemed to turn red and rather quickly it was dark. To help themselves feel brave, the little monkeys shouted a new version of their song:

We don't believe in crocodile,
There's no such beast as crocodile.

Suku flew to Giraffe. 'Look down there.' Together they peered at the moonlit river bank. Down it slid a long, dark shadow.

'Trouble,' muttered Twiga. 'Come on.'

The dark shadow slid into the water. Long slow ripples spread over the surface. Monkeys laughed. It made their heads look very wide and their shoulders very narrow. More and more ripples came.

Tip found his mouth going dry when a large log-like thing moved slowly across the river. Wide-eyed they watched it disappear into the shadows.

'Ooooooff,' said Top. 'That was scary.'

They peered into the water which now was calm again. 'Our faces look very pale.' There was a tremble in Tip's voice.

'It's only the m-m-oonlight,' whispered Top. 'Come on let's sing.'

With a tremble in their voices they started:

Crocodiles, crocodiles,
We don't believe in crocodiles.

'You don't, *eh?*' came a loud thundery voice from behind them. 'So much the better for me.'

Tip saw a great, wide-open mouth and two beady little eyes. Top gaped at deadly rows of teeth. Hot breath that smelt of swamps and stale meat swirled around them. The little monkeys huddled together in terror anchored by those beady eyes. Crocodile slithered closer and closer.

'I don't exist, *eh?*' thundered the voice. 'Right then. Neither will you!' Crocodile shuffled closer and opened his mouth wider. He took no notice of the galloping noise which had become louder. Then he shot forward and his huge jaws crunched together.

But Crocodile's mouth was *empty.* A split second before it slammed shut, Twiga's strong neck had swept down, carrying two small terrified monkeys to safety.

'Near thing,' panted Giraffe. 'I was just in time.'

'It was all true about the beady eyes and the teeth and the ...' Tip and Top hugged Twiga's neck. '*Oh,* thank you for saving us.'

The camp fire was only a red glow. Nobody said a word.

Daudi stood up. 'The monkeys got away with it, but people won't. If we say there are no crocodiles we are dangerously wrong. And if we say we have not sinned we deceive ourselves. But make no mistake, sin is much, much more deadly than crocodiles. Isn't it wonderful that God says if we admit we are sinners he forgives our sins and makes us thoroughly clean from all our wrongdoing?'

* * *

What's Inside the Fable?

Special Message: Don't deceive yourself. To pretend sin isn't real, is deadly dangerous.

Read *John's first letter, chapter 1 verses 8 to 10.*

Don't be deceived. You can't make a fool of God.

Read *Galatians chapter 6 verses 7 to 10.*

Jesus told a story explaining this. *Luke chapter 18 verses 9 to 14.*

6

SAFE AS POISON

Daudi wrote in the dust: Numbers 3223.

'Truly,' said those that listened, 'two and three are numbers.'

'And so are three and two,' replied Daudi. 'Thirty-two is also a number as is twenty-three. The whole thing is a riddle. Listen with open ears.'

There was danger in the roots of the great *buyu* tree, for Nzoka, the snake, lived there with his wife and family of little poison-fanged snakelets. Now Nzoka always had a famine within him. He complained to his wife. 'There is never enough food here to satisfy a grown snake's stomach.'

Her tongue shot out like forked lightning. 'Why not seek your own supplies?'

Nzoka hissed. 'I will get my food in my own way. My stomach demands it.'

His wife bared her fangs. 'Be careful, you stupid serpent. You'll wriggle into trouble. Your wisdom ceases where your stomach begins.'

Snake uncoiled smoothly. 'No creature in the jungle has my cunning. Me in trouble?' He sneered as he slid out of the roots of the *buyu* tree and wriggled his way in the warm dust towards the house of Perembi, the hunter.

Now Perembi's son had a hen called Kuku. She had laid an egg inside the hunter's house and was singing her song to announce it. Nzoka glided towards the house. The mud plaster of the wall had been broken away at the bottom and there was a place through which he could squeeze his body. As Kuku cackled and cackled, Nzoka's mouth watered and gurgles made their way from deep within him.

He came to the hole in the wall, squeezed his body through the gap, and in he went. And there was the egg – large, warm, comforting-looking, just right to bring satisfaction to any snake's inside. He wanted that egg more than anything else. Mouth open wide he slowly slid forward and – *wuumph* – the egg became a bulge just south of his neck. He wriggled

happily to the wall. His head went through and some of his neck, but there the bulge stopped him. Nzoka smiled slyly and bumped the lump against the sides of the hole. The shell cracked and broke. '*Ooh, aah,* lovely!' His interior was filled with satisfaction. Filled with content, he squeezed the rest of his body through the hole and the egg squelched comfortingly down his supple body. With a smug smile he wriggled back amongst the roots of the *buyu* tree to be met by his wife.

She hissed. 'What have you been doing? Where have you been? What trouble are you in?'

Yawning, Nzoka twitched his tail. 'Silence, she-serpent, I know what I'm doing. And my stomach now sings as it never sang with your cooking inside it.' He closed his eyes but she went on.

'You be careful. You'll be found out.' Poison dribbled from her lips.

Nzoka smiled a small smile. His stomach was at peace. His wife was full of words but he was full of egg.

Next day, again he heard the song of Kuku the hen. Again he found the hole in the wall. Again he crawled through that hole, swallowed the egg, and yet again his stomach was flooded with joy as he passed through the gap in the wall.

Later, seeing him lying curled and content his wife said, 'Be careful, oh Snake. There's trouble round the corner for you. Do things such as you're doing and you'll be caught.' But Nzoka closed his ears to the sound of her voice, choosing rather the contented murmur of his stomach.

On the third day he listened for the song of the hen. He believed himself so safe that he didn't even bother to look this way and that. In he went. Down

went the egg and again his stomach rejoiced within him. Again his wife warned him with many words. He bared his fangs. 'Stop nagging. There is no danger in this, I tell you.'

Day followed day. Egg followed egg. Each day he was less cautious. 'Danger!' scoffed Snake as he snoozed off to sleep. Never was there a safer or simpler way of living. But even as he was saying it the son of Perembi said, 'My father, daily I hear the singing of Kuku but she sings without result. See, there is the place she lays.'

'There is no egg, my son. But there are the tracks of Snake.'

Together they worked out a plan. In the morning when Kuku laid her egg and sang Nzoka followed his custom. He forced his way through the sticks, swallowed the egg, cracked the bulge behind his neck and glided off to the *buyu* tree.

Perembi's son watched everything he did and in his mind a plan grew. Inside the *buyu* tree, Snake's wife said to her children, 'Here comes your gluttonous father who follows the way of small wisdom, the way of danger, the way that will lead to trouble, to discovery, to ...'

Nzoka hissed horribly and beat at his wife with his tail.

'Silence, wordy serpent.'

Perembi and his son, Mbili, thought deep thoughts and the boy's plan made his father laugh aloud. Early next morning they took an egg and placed it in water in a clay pot over the fire. The water boiled and the egg became harder and harder.

Kuku settled on her nest and after a time started to cackle. In the roots of the *buyu* tree Nzoka heard her and started to smile hungrily. But his wife hissed, 'Don't deceive yourself. You'll get caught. It'll be the end of you.' But Nzoka took no notice.

With a wooden spoon Mbili exchanged eggs. Each looked the same but only Mbili and his father knew how different they were.

Nzoka shot through the hole in the wall, his eyes fixed on the egg. He smiled his snaky smile. 'Danger? Where is there danger?'

If he had looked at the top of the grain bin he would have seen the eyes of Perembi and Mbili. Had he been able to see behind the bin he would have seen a knobbed stick firmly gripped in the boy's hand. But Nzoka had eyes only for the egg for which his stomach called greedily. As usual he swallowed it. '*Yoh!*' he thought to himself. 'Perhaps Kuku, the hen, has fever today. This egg is hot.' His head as

usual went easily through the hole in the wall but his neck stuck. He bumped the hard-boiled egg against the sticks but nothing happened. He banged harder and harder but the egg would not break. Fear gripped him. In a frenzy Nzoka squirmed with his head and lashed with his tail but the hard-boiled egg anchored him.

'*Ah*,' chuckled Perembi, 'it seemed so safe to you, oh Snake.'

Mbili gripped his knobbed stick. 'Egg thief! You thought it was safe because you did it so often.' He came from behind the grain bin and – WALLOP!

At sunset the wife of Nzoka, who had taken her snakelets for their evening wriggle, hissed, 'Look over towards the rubbish heap.'

They all watched the body of Nzoka departing in the mouth of Mbisi, the hyena. 'Listen, you snakelets, do not follow the ways of your father. He said there was no danger. Because he had done it again and again he said it was safe. But look at him now.'

The flickering light from the camp fire showed up a great buyu tree behind them. Mboga turned up the wick of the hurricane lantern. 'Great one, I have read that verse: Numbers 32:23. it says, "Be sure your sin will find you out."'

'Right,' said Daudi. 'Words to remember. And every time you look at an egg you can remember the story of Nzoka, the snake, whose sin found him out. But more important, remember that the Lord Jesus Christ came to take the poison out of sin for everyone who will trust their life into his care and go his way.'

* * *

What's Inside the Fable?

Special Message: Sin is deadly.

Read *Romans chapter 6 verse 23* and then *Romans 6 verses 1 to 22.*

7

KEEP THEM FLYING

Nyani pushed his thumb against the limb of the *buyu* tree and again a *dudu* died. The grandfather of many monkeys was filled with scorching anger. He chattered loudly as he climbed through the limbs of his favourite *buyu* tree. He swung by his tail and confided his troubles to Twiga, the giraffe.

'Twiga, there are *dudus* of the worst sort in this *buyu* tree. Everyone has fleas, ticks are irritating, but at least respectable; but lice ... no!' He shuddered, wrinking his nose and scratching vigorously at the very thought.

Twiga listened with sympathy, moistening his lips with his long black tongue. 'I should think the roosting of vultures on the limbs of your family tree is the cause of your trouble.'

Nyani ground his monkey teeth. 'That bird of disgusting ways, that eater of things long dead, that … that …' words failed him but he continued to chatter angrily.

Twiga remarked mildly. 'Show a little fierceness, Nyani, and it's unlikely that vultures will alight on your *buyu* tree.'

Nyani listened with interest and scratched thoughtfully.

Twiga went on, 'You can't stop them flying over your *buyu* tree but you can stop them from roosting there.'

Nyani thought for a while and the matter slowly became clear to his monkey mind. At once he set about collecting stones to be kept in the hollow limb for use if vultures should trouble him again.

Daudi threw some sticks on the camp fire. A shower of sparks lit up the faces of his listeners.

'I'll give you a clue. You can't stop them flying over but you can stop them roosting.'

'I have it,' shouted Mboga. 'It's temptation. For Shaitan – the devil – to whisper in your ear is not sin but to stop and listen is a different matter.'

Daudi nodded slowly, 'Truly. But remember temptation is not sin. You can't stop the devil's voice from reaching your ears but to take notice of what he suggests and do it – that is sin.'

* * *

What's Inside the Fable?

Special message: Temptation, if overcome, helps Christians to grow strong.

Read *James chapter 1 verses 2-4.*

8

THE SMALL WISDOM OF FEEDING VULTURES

'Bwana Daudi,' asked Mboga, 'what's the medicine for overcoming temptation?'

Daudi, who had a bucketful of cough mixture, nodded slowly. 'I'll dispense that at tonight's campfire.'

Nyani had two small monkey nephews, Kibo and Saba, who listened to what he had to tell them. Kibo let the words go right through his head but Saba used his ears wisely.

Now Nyani hated vultures and the *dudus* that lived so happily amongst their feathers. But if these insects that crawled and bit happened to find their way on to monkeys they brought no joy. Nyani waved his arms excitedly. 'Keep away from vultures and keep them away from you.'

Saba nodded slowly. He had once been bitten by lice and didn't want it to happen again. Also the scrawny necks of vultures and their unclean claws brought him no joy.

'Pelt them with stones,' shouted Nyani. 'It will bring strength to your throwing arm and keep trouble from your tree.'

Kibo smiled. 'Horrible birds, uncle, aren't they? I hate them too.' But the truth was that he was fascinated by their sharp beaks, their featherless necks and the way their tails swayed.

One day a vulture circled in the sky, muttering to itself, 'Is there anything dead round here?' He went to have a look at Saba's tree. Seeing him coming in to land, Saba went to the hollow in the tree where he stored stones. At once he threw some hard and straight. Vulture lost a few feathers and squawked as he flew away. But before long he returned to be met by a second shower of stones. Scuttling out of range he flapped heavily into the air and landed close to Kibo's tree.

Monkey's eyes drank in every movement. He looked this way and that and seeing his uncle in the distance, yelled, 'Go away! Go away!' He threw stones nowhere near Vulture, and some bones which landed at the great bird's feet. Kibo thought, 'Why shouldn't I play a game with him just for kicks?'

Next day two vultures came. Kibo chuckled. 'This is rather fun. They may have dangerous-looking

beaks and sharp-looking claws but really, there's no danger.'

That day he threw more bones than stones. Next day three vultures came. 'Away with you,' shouted Kibo. 'Clear out. On your way, chickens.'

There was an admiring sound in Vulture's husky voice, 'You're an experienced monkey. There's nothing of the chicken about you.'

 Kibo started to feel warm inside. He muttered, 'He's right. And what's more, I can stop this game whenever I want to.'

The vultures looked knowingly at each other and whispered down their hooked beaks. 'He's coming our way. See, he's throwing bones today but not a single stone.'

Twiga, the giraffe, looked over the top of the umbrella tree and saw all that was happening. He shouted, 'Monkey, you can't stop them flying over or under you but watch out. Throw stones, *stones*, do you hear me? Not bones.'

But Kibo took no notice. A week went by. The vultures now came right up to the foot of the tree. Kibo's eyes were hot as he looked at them. His mouth was dry and he felt a tiny bit scared.

The day came when a dozen vultures walked around his tree, their eyes fixed on him. Kibo felt monkey perspiration on his upper lip but he shrugged and told himself, 'Everybody else does it, and anyway I'm too smart to be caught. Things are under control. When it comes to handling vultures I know my way around.'

But even as he said it, the air was full of the sound of vultures' wings above him, below him, around him. A flight of vultures circled slowly, looking at him with hungry eyes. 'It's a game just for kicks,' croaked one imitating Kibo's voice. 'Everybody does it, and anyhow I'm too smart to be caught,' jeered another.

The largest vulture of them all squawked huskily, 'Get on with it. We're hungry. It's meat we want, not bones.' He landed on Kibo's tree. His claws were strong and sharp.

Another and another followed, their beaks eager. 'GO AWAY,' shrieked monkey. This time he meant it from the bottom of his heart. But still vultures came from all directions. They shuffled closer and closer. Kibo trembled with fear. Through his mind scurried the thought, 'Stop them landing. I must stop them landing. Throw stones. I must throw stones.' But before he could do a thing he was surrounded with clutching claws and hooked beaks that snapped hungrily. Terrified he grabbed a stick and swung it wildly. Through his mind rang Twiga's warning, 'Keep them flying. Keep them flying. Don't let them land. They're vile. They're deadly.'

Great ominous wings flapped around him. Evil-smelling feathers brushed against his face as the vultures moved closer. Horrible screeching filled the jungle. Kibo's voice came thinly from the tangle of vicious birds, 'Go away. Go away. Go ...'

At sunset the vultures had gone. Twiga and Nyani came slowly to Kibo's tree. They saw all that remained of little monkey – a pile of bones – his bones.

Giraffe shook his head. 'That's the way of vultures. Encourage them, or still worse, feed them, then more come and take over and destroy.'

On the other side of the hill Saba filled up the hollow in his tree with stones. He was determined to fight any vultures that came near his tree and his throwing arm was stronger than it had ever been.

Daudi leant forward. 'Is the matter clear? Temptation, testing, comes to everybody. Jesus himself was tempted but he did not sin and he showed us how to deal with it. A thought comes into your mind suggesting you do something wrong. Say NO, and you're strengthened to resist the next test. But suppose you allow that thought into your imagination? It will grow into a desire which blossoms into an action. That action is sin, and sin in the long run always ends in disaster.'

* * *

What's Inside the Fable?

Special Message: Temptation and testing is a friend when you resist it.

Read how Jesus was tempted and how he overcame the devil in *Matthew chapter 4 verses 1 to 11*. He used the Word of God.

Read *Psalm 119 verse 11*.

9
MONKEY IN THE LION'S SKIN

After sunset Mbogo lit the camp fire.

'Some people try to deceive both God and people but it doesn't work,' said Daudi. 'Listen to the story of a monkey who ...'

Mboga laughed. 'The one who stole the lion skin?'

'That's the one.'

Tutu, the monkey, sat up in the umbrella tree thoughtfully eating green caterpillars. He watched the hunter's wife spread a lion's skin in the sun to drive out the many-legged *dudus* that made their home in it. He saw the hunter's son pick up the skin and wrap it round himself and scare the other children of the village.

Tutu's eyes gleamed as a monkey idea grew in his head. 'If I am in a lion's skin I shall be a lion. I shall become a new creature.'

He leapt from his hiding place, snatched the skin from the boy, and bolted off into the jungle. Ahead was a hollow *buyu* tree with a large hole in its trunk. Tutu wrapped the lion's skin tightly round him, put his head through the hole and roared in a voice he hoped was like lion's.

Budi, the bat, and his large tribe spent the day time in the darkness of that hollow tree. Tutu's roar sounded like thunder. He giggled. 'That will bring fear to the hearts of many bats, for they will think I am a lion. Who but a lion can be in a lion's skin?'

Budi certainly had fear for he well remembered when as a batlet he had heard the same noise and had seen a great paw groping inside the cave where he lived. For Simba, the lion, had an enquiring mind and wondered why the winged animals slept feet up and heads down. In panic a cloud of bats poured into the sunlight, their darkness-loving eyes dazzled by the glare.

Tutu was delighted. He told himself, 'I'm different and important and awe-inspiring in my new skin.'

Hyena was asleep under a thorn bush. His nose suddenly told him: Lion – beware! There was a strong smell of monkey but that part of the jungle was riddled with monkeys. He did not look. His nose had warned him and he well knew that the legs of Hyena are shorter than those of Lion. Tutu was delighted as he watched the scavenger of the jungle creep into his lair. He wriggled with importance inside the ill-fitting skin and chuckled, 'Hyena thought I was a lion. My new skin makes all the difference.'

Suku, the parrot, was perched in the umbrella tree. He squawked, 'What will happen when you meet a bad-tempered rhino or a hungry leopard, *eh*? Think of it. What will you do then?'

But Tutu wasn't listening. His monkey mind was working on the problem of how to make the lion's skin fit better. For hours he was busy rubbing some of the tougher places with the inside of a coconut. Then he pinned the skin carefully in place with long, strong thorns, wriggling till he was less uncomfortable. He told himself, 'Now everyone will see that I'm a lion and they'll run for their lives.'

He paraded up and down the jungle path practising his roaring and then – up the *buyu* tree again, round a limb went his tail and he swung happily to and fro.

Boohoo, the hippo, snoozed in the water-lily pond. His eyes opened slowly. He blinked. '*Um* – unusual. Is this – an *–um* – nightmare?' He waddled out of the water and called to his tall friend, the giraffe. 'Twiga, do lions climb trees?'

'Yes, Boohoo. Lions often climb trees. I've seen Simba, the lion, sprawled out on a branch sunning himself.'

'Oh, good. I just saw a lion in a tree. He was swinging by his tail.'

'He was what?'

'Swinging by his tail.'

'Boohoo, lions climb trees but they don't swing by their tails.'

'This one did. I saw him. Come over and see for yourself. This way. Move quietly. Now look up there. See, it has a long tail and a shaggy mane. It's a lion. Let's run before he eats us.'

Twiga smiled. 'He won't eat us. Good morning there.'

The voice from up the tree said, '*Er, oh*, R-O-A-R. Don't come any closer to this tree or I'll leap from this branch and tear you to bits. I'm the king of the beasts – a lion!'

Boohoo gulped. '*Er*, I know that voice. It isn't lion. It – *er – um* ...'

'It certainly isn't lion,' agreed Twiga. He called to monkey, 'Tutu, take off that moth-eaten lion skin. You'll suffocate.'

'Don't talk to me like that, Giraffe. I'm not a monkey any more. I've become a lion.' He roared and snarled. 'But don't you understand? A new skin makes a new animal.'

Giraffe answered patiently, 'You can wear the hide of Rhino but inside you'll still be a monkey. You may wear the feathers of Ostrich but you won't become a bird. You may crawl right into the skin of Nzoka, the snake, and hiss horribly but you'll still remain plain monkey.'

Tutu giggled. 'But did you see Hyena run, Twiga? He thought I was a lion. The skin deceived ...'

'You may fool dazzled bats and hyenas who run before they look but to wear a new skin is not to change you. You need to be all new to be a new creature ...' Giraffe was peering thoughtfully at the large rocks on the side of a small hill. 'Boohoo, sometimes the best way to teach monkey anything is to let him do what he wants and find out for himself.'

They heard Suku, the parrot, screech in alarm. 'I smell danger,' breathed Twiga. 'Up in those rocks.'

Boohoo lifted up his big nostrils. '*Mmmm*, all I can smell is Leopard. Oh – Leopard. Tutu, run! Leopard's coming.'

'I'm not running away from a leopard – not this lion.' He roared huskily and was answered by a spine-chilling growl.

'Stand back,' ordered Tutu. 'I am a lion. King of the beasts. I'm fierce and ferocious. I'll ...'

Leopard growled and sprang. In a twinkling the jungle saw the strange sight of an oddly-shaped lion scuttling up a tree just ahead of the deadly claws of Chewi, the leopard. Tutu climbed so fast that the lion's skin fell off.

Boohoo blinked. '*Um* – nasty situation that. Do you think he realises now that he's only a monkey?'

'He should,' nodded Twiga. 'He should learn a lot clinging to the highest, thinnest limb of the *buyu* tree with a fierce and hungry leopard less than a hippo's length behind him.'

Daudi lit his hurricane lantern from the glowing embers of the fire.

'Is the matter understood? It's becoming a member of God's family that makes you new. There are no two ways about it. Patched-up lives are no good to God. It's not repairs that you need. It's forgiveness.'

* * *

What's Inside the Fable?

Special Message: Becoming a Christian starts a new life – everlasting life.

Read *2 Corinthians chapter 5 verses 17 and 18.*

Jesus can give us life because he came back to life. *Colossians chapter 3 verses 1 to 4.* Keep reading in the same chapter, *verses 12 to 17,* to see how to live this new life.

10
LITTLE LEOPARDS BECOME BIG LEOPARDS

'Leopards,' said Daudi, 'are kali – fierce.'

Mgogo, who never missed a camp fire story, reached for his knobbed stick. 'Yoh! Their teeth, their claws, the way they can climb, the look in their eye ...' He shivered.

'Eheh,' said Daudi, 'but their skins are beautiful and valuable to hunters who sell those skins for much money in the market place. Listen to the story of little leopards and big leopards.'

Perembi, the hunter, moved silently through the jungle. The wind blew in his face. In his right hand was a bow, on his back a quiver of arrows, at his side a hunting knife. Grasped in his left hand was his hunting spear. He walked up-wind, his eyes probing every shadow and bush. Suddenly he stopped. He saw movement. He fitted arrow to bow string and then spat with disgust. A zebra moved out into the sunlight. Zebra is an animal of small profit to any hunter.

That day Perembi hoped to find and kill Chewi, the leopard, whose skin was worth many cows. He moved on. The thornbush around him made the light appear mottled, streaked and striped. His eyes were as keen as his spear. A leopard could melt into such a background and not be seen until his strong teeth and claws had done great damage.

Perembi moved into the shadow of a tree and froze into silent stillness. He had seen a movement. He looked up. It was only Twiga, the giraffe, whose body toned with the light and shade. Again Perembi spat

and continued on his hunter's way. Then he stopped. The arrow he chose from his quiver was the sharpest. He moved behind the great trunk of a *buyu* tree, his spear ready to hand, for there, lying on a rock in the sun was Chewi, the leopard. He fitted the arrow to the bow string. His eyes sparkled when he saw the leopard was of great size. The spots on his skin were clearly marked.

'Here,' thought Perembi, 'could be great profit.'

Twang! The arrow sped. He leapt behind the *buyu* tree and came out on the other side, spear held in one hand, hunting knife in the other. He was tense, expectant, but slowly he relaxed. A smile came over his face for the arrow had sped truly and leopard lay dead, his great muscles twitching.

Perembi tested the edge of his hunting knife on his thumb. Skinning a leopard called for special skill. The sun beat down. Sweat ran into his eyes.

There was a strange sound and the grass rustled behind him. He felt the hair on the back of his head stand up straight. He gripped the spear and turned, and there, not two paces away was another leopard. Perembi slashed the trunk of a thorn tree, stripped off a length of bark and tied it gently round the body of the leopard which was the smallest that he had ever seen.

He relaxed and chuckled, 'Little one, you're coming home with me and will they not say, 'He is the greatest of hunters'? Two leopards with one arrow!'

He strode back to his house, a magnificent leopard skin over one shoulder and little leopard over the other. As he entered his village amongst the buyu trees he sang his song of success. Many came to greet him. The children shouted with laughter and amazement when they saw little leopard.

Perembi said, 'Is he not a beautiful baby animal? See, his claws are very small, his teeth are tiny and I think his eyes are the kindest I have ever seen in the jungle. Look after him properly,' he told the children. 'He will be your pet and he will never be fierce if you feed him only on porridge.'

They shouted with joy. 'We will follow your words, Great One.'

Hearing the laughter and shouting the chief, who was the greatest hunter in the whole jungle, came to greet Perembi and praise his skill. Then he saw the group of laughing children. He stopped and lifted his spear.

'*Yoh!* A little leopard.'

Perembi explained, but the chief shook his head. 'A little leopard is not a creature of peace to have in the village. Behold, little leopards become big leopards and big leopards kill.'

But the children implored him. 'Great one, do not kill our little leopard. See, it has tender eyes. See how it eats its porridge from our hands. Its claws are too small to cause harm. And its teeth – *yoh!* they're tiny!'

The hunter added his word. 'Great One, it can do no harm. It's but a little leopard.'

'Truly,' said the great chief, 'but it is also true that little leopards become big leopards and big leopards kill. Follow the way of wisdom and let me kill it now before anyone is hurt.'

But they refused with strong words.

Day by day the children fed little leopard on porridge and it grew. Its teeth grew. Its claws grew. Its spots grew but it had the kindest eyes ever seen in the jungle. The children played with it. It had no anger at the roughness of even the very smallest children. Its tail would often be pulled, its ears too.

But still there was kindness in its eyes and daily at the hour of food they fed it on porridge.

Month followed month. Its teeth grew longer. Its claws grew longer and even the spots on its skin became larger. One morning the chief came to the house of Perembi. Out from the hunter's *kaya* walked little leopard, now half-grown. The chief stepped back, his hand on his hunting knife.

At once there were many loud noises. 'Great One, put your knife back. Behold, this is our tame little leopard, fed only on porridge. See the kindness in its eyes. It's a creature of safety. It's the plaything of the children.'

But the chief shook his head. 'Porridge or no porridge, plaything of the children it may be, but do not deceive yourselves. Little leopards become big leopards and big leopards kill.'

'*Koh!*' said Perembi, rolling the leopard over with his foot and scratching it with his big toe. The animal purred deeply and wriggled in delight. 'There is no fear in this little leopard.' The hunter glared at the chief. 'Others, certainly, but not this one. It's always been fed on porridge.'

The chief spoke quietly, 'You have heard my words. It is the nature of leopards to kill.'

But those of Perembi's family took no notice and daily they fed the leopard. It's teeth continued to grow. Its claws continued to grow, and week by week it became larger and larger but its eyes were kind and did not lose their kindness even when four children rode upon it and steered it with its tail. But there were those in the village who shook their heads and said, '*Yoh!* it has become a great beast.' But Perembi only laughed. 'Truly, but it's been fed only on porridge. There is no fierceness in our leopard.'

Time went by. Leopard ate porridge in great quantity and its teeth grew until they were longer than those which hung around the neck of witch-doctor. Its claws were longer and sharper than the great wait-a-bit thorns of the jungle. Its spots were black and clear-cut against its golden-coloured skin. Its long tail moved with grace and its eyes were the kindest in the jungle...

Until one morning the youngest son of the household wandered down the path which led to the well. As he walked, the limb of a thornbush reached out and scratched his leg. A great red drop trickled down the leg and large tears welled from the eyes of the child.

Hearing his sadness, Chewi ran down the track. His long red tongue slid past his great white teeth. Gently he licked the bleeding leg. Then it happened. Big leopard snarled. His eyes narrowed to cruel, steely slits. The taste of blood called wildly to something deep within him. He knocked the child out of his way.

Chewi turned and walked slowly back to the hunter's house, the muscles rippling beneath his spotted skin, his long sharp claws twitching, his lips drawn back from his long white teeth. The first snarl, ever, creased the grown leopard's face, lighted by cold, cruel, steely eyes.

Inside his house Perembi was making new arrows, whittling skilfully with his hunting knife. In the shadow he saw Chewi glide into the house. He shouted, 'Clear out!' as he bent his head to pick up an arrow shaft. In that second Chewi struck with tooth and claw. Perembi grabbed for his hunting knife but the fight was over before he could even grip it.

Little leopard had become big leopard and big leopard had killed.

Screams of alarm rang through the village. People fled in all directions and doors were slammed and locked. Leopard stalked between the silent African houses. The chief moved out to meet him, spear in hand. Quietly he said, 'I warned them. Now big leopard will kill and keep on killing unless ...'

The wild beast hurled itself fiercely into the attack, fighting viciously with ripping claws and tearing fangs. The battle was long and bitter. At last the leopard lay dead but the chief was wounded in both his hands, both his feet and his side.

Rejoicing, the villagers came out of hiding. The chief told them, 'There's nothing to fear now. The leopard is dead. But so, too, is Perembi for he chose to take no notice of my warning that little leopards become big leopards and big leopards kill.'

Daudi looked into the camp fire for a moment and then, 'This is a double riddle. What was the name of the great chief and what was the name of the leopard?'

Mgogo jumped up, in his eagerness upsetting his stool. 'The name of the leopard was sin because little sins become big sins and sins, big or small, kill. And the name of the Great Chief was the Lord Jesus Christ, the son of God, for he was wounded in both hands, both feet and his side. He died so that we could be forgiven.'

'Truly,' agreed Daudi. 'The Bible tells us, "He was pierced for our rebellion, he was crushed for our sins. The punishment that brought us peace was upon him and by his wounds we are healed. The Lord has laid on him the sin of us all." '

Mgogo said quietly, so quietly that only Daudi heard, 'By his wounds I am healed.'

* * *

What's Inside the Fable?

Special Message: Little sins become big sins. Jesus died so that we might be forgiven.

Read *Ephesians 1:7*.

Read *Isaiah 53:5*.

EPILOGUE
THE MILK IN THE COCONUT

Mgogo sat quietly as Daudi measured out medicines. He put them in a large bucket and stirred with a huge wooden spoon. The African boy smiled, 'Bwana Daudi, last night I had a dream. Nyani and his many relations visited me as I slept. It was a thing of amazement.

'I could see the old monkey sitting on a big rock while five monkeys of small wisdom squabbled on an invisible branch of a *buyu* tree.' Mgogo grinned. 'Great one, it was one of those strange dreams for I could see the moon shining through the bodies of Toto, Tip and Top, Koko and Tutu.'

Daudi laughed. 'I know that sort of dream. What happened?'

Nyani was speaking, 'In the village of the tail-less ones there was one called Mgogo who rejoiced to hear stories of those of us who live in the jungle. He heard how you, Toto, could not climb over the wall called sin.'

Toto rubbed the back of his neck. *'I fell from a height. It was a wall of no joy.'*

'You realised that sin separates you from God?' asked Daudi.

Mgogo nodded. 'I did. But listen to the rest of my dream.'

Nyani looked further down the invisible limb. 'And he heard of you, Koko, and what happened with that coconut in the swamp.'

'Truly, oh Nyani,' Koko murmured, 'there was small profit in your monkey idea to save myself from that terrible, down-sucking mud.'

Nyani suddenly became interested in the tip of his tail.

Mgogo leaned across to Daudi and whispered, 'I had fear when I realised that nothing I could do would help me against the deadliness of sin.'

Daudi nodded and the boy went on.

'Yoh?' questioned Tip and Top, 'and did he hear that we didn't believe in crocodiles?'

Nyani nodded solemnly. 'He heard and his blood turned to water. For though he believed in both crocodiles and what is worse than crocodiles, he did not know how to escape.'

'My joy was small,' shivered Mgogo. 'My sin worried me. I tried to forget it but my memory kept reminding me that sin's teeth were more deadly than crocodile's.

'Then when I heard of Tutu and the lion skin, I realised I had to repent – to change my mind about the way I was going. So I asked Jesus to forgive me and to make me a new person. I wanted him to blot out my sin.'

'And what did you do?' asked Daudi.

'I asked him to blot mine out as a man rubs out footprints in the sand. He did.'

Daudi interrupted, 'You saw the scars in his feet? You thought of the cost of the cross to him?'

There was a long silence then Mgogo smiled. 'Today I have thought of my dream and of your stories. Truly there is no profit in monkey wisdom but there is great happiness and joy, for I am out of the swamp and on the right side of the wall. I am a new person.'

Daudi nodded. 'Remember, your soul must grow now. Feed it daily.' He tapped the Bible on the table before him. 'If you would live with happiness keep clear of little leopards and avoid feeding vultures. Live with your eyes on Jesus.'

'Is not life like a coconut?' asked Mgogo. 'It is but monkey wisdom for anyone who belongs to Jesus to continue chewing the shell when he has found that inside is milk and meat.'

GLOSSARY

JUNGLE DOCTOR'S WORDS AND NAMES
How to say them and what they mean

Animals	Pronunciation
Budi - bat	Boodee
Chewi - leopard	Chewee
Chibwa - dog	Cheebwer
Kibo - monkey	Keeboe
Koko - monkey	Cocoa
Kuku - hen	Kookoo
Mbisi - hyena	Mbeesee
Moto - monkey	Mowtoe
Nyani - monkey	Nyahnee
Nzoka - snake	Nzoker
Saba - monkey	Sarbar
Simba - lion	Simber
Suku - parrot	Sookoo
Toto - monkey twin	Toetoe
Tutu - monkey	Tootoo
Twiga - giraffe	Twigger

Names	Pronunciation	English
Daudi	Dhawdee	David
Goha	Goha	Spear
Mabwe	Marbway	Stone
Mbili	Mbilee	Two
Mbogo	Mbowger	Vegetable
Mdimi	Mdeemee	Shepherd
Mgoga	Mmgogoe	Person from the Gogo tribe
Mgulu	Mgooloo	Leg
Perembi	Perembee	Hunter
Shaitan	Shaytan	Satan

Swahili	Pronunciation	English
Buyu	Booyoo	Baobab tree
Bwana	Bwarner	Sir, Mister, Lord
Dudu	Doodoo	Insect
Eheh	Ayhay	Agreement (with nod of head)
Kali	Karlee	Fierce
Koh	Koe	*Exclamation
Matope	Martoepay	Mud
Ng'o	Ngoe	No
Yoh	Yoe	Exclamation (please raise the eyebrows)

* (tone of voice will indicate amazement, surprise or disgust)

CHRISTIAN FOCUS PUBLICATIONS

F **H** **·K·** **m**

| Christian | Christian | CF4K | Mentor |
| Focus | Heritage | | |

Christian Focus Publications publishes books for adults and children under its four main imprints: Christian Focus, CF4K, Mentor and Christian Heritage. Our books reflect that God's word is reliable and Jesus is the way to know him, and live for ever with him.

Our children's publication list includes a Sunday School curriculum that covers pre-school to early teens; puzzle and activity books. We also publish personal and family devotional titles, biographies and inspirational stories that children will love.

If you are looking for quality Bible teaching for children then we have an excellent range of Bible story and age specific theological books.

From pre-school to teenage fiction, we have it covered!

Find us at our web page:
www.christianfocus.com

CF4·K
Because you're never
too young to know Jesus